Rosalie
the Rapunzel
Fairy

To Harper Ribeiro, with love from the fairies

Special thanks to Rachel Elliot

Copyright © 2016 by Rainbow Magic Limited.

All rights reserved. Published by Scholastic Inc., *Publishers since 1920.* SCHOLASTIC and associated logos are trademarks and/or registered trademarks of Scholastic Inc. RAINBOW MAGIC is a trademark of Rainbow Magic Limited. Reg. U.S. Patent & Trademark Office and other countries. HIT and the HIT logo are trademarks of HIT Entertainment Limited.

The publisher does not have any control over and does not assume any responsibility for author or third-party websites or their content.

No part of this publication may be reproduced, stored in a retrieval system, or transmitted in any form or by any means, electronic, mechanical, photocopying, recording, or otherwise, without written permission of the publisher. For information regarding permission, write to Scholastic Inc., Attention: Permissions Department, 557 Broadway, New York, NY 10012.

This book is a work of fiction. Names, characters, places, and incidents are either the product of the author's imagination or are used fictitiously, and any resemblance to actual persons, living or dead, business establishments, events, or locales is entirely coincidental.

ISBN 978-1-338-05502-3

10 9 8 7 6 5 4 3 2 1   17 18 19 20 21

Printed in the U.S.A.   40
First edition, March 2017

Rosalie
the Rapunzel
Fairy

by Daisy Meadows

SCHOLASTIC INC.

The Fairyland Palace

Fairyland Library

The Three Bears' Cottage

Island

Thumbelina's Cottage

Storybook World

Rapunzel's Tower

Red Riding Hood's Grandmother's House

Red Riding Hood Woods

The fairies want stories to stay just the same.
But I've planned a funny and mischievous game.
I'll change all their tales without further ado,
By adding some tricks and a goblin or two!

The four magic stories will soon be improved
When everything that's nice and sweet is removed.
Their dull happy endings are ruined and lost,
For no one's as smart as handsome Jack Frost!

Contents

Intruder in the Tower

"Hurry up, Kirsty," called Rachel Walker, skipping past colorful bunting and festival tents. "I can't wait to get to the Story Barge."

Her best friend, Kirsty Tate, had paused to look at a tent that was decorated with the first lines of lots of different children's books. She grinned at Rachel and ran to catch up to her.

"That tent is amazing," she said. "I want to make sure I go back later and see how many first lines I recognize."

Rachel and Kirsty were having a wonderful weekend. Rachel was staying with Kirsty so that they could go to the Wetherbury Storytelling Festival together. One of their favorite authors, Alana

Yarn, was leading the festival and had arranged lots of fun storytelling activities.

"We did so much yesterday, it feels like we've had a whole weekend already," said Rachel. "There was the *Goldilocks* puppet show and Alana's storytelling performance of *Thumbelina*."

"And we met the Storybook Fairies," Kirsty added, remembering the magical adventures they had shared with Elle the Thumbelina Fairy and Mariana the Goldilocks Fairy.

"And we still have all of Sunday ahead of us," said Rachel, stopping to do a cartwheel. "I'm so excited! I wonder what Alana has planned for today."

"I hope we see the Storybook Fairies again," Kirsty added.

"I'm sure we will," said Rachel. "After all, there are still two magical objects to find."

The girls were secret friends of Fairyland, but this was the first time that they had met the Storybook Fairies. Elle the Thumbelina Fairy had asked Rachel and Kirsty to help them because Jack Frost had stolen their magical objects. Rachel and Kirsty had already helped Elle and Mariana get their magical objects back, but Rosalie the Rapunzel Fairy and Ruth the Red Riding Hood Fairy were still missing theirs.

The river was sparkling in the sunshine, and as they got closer to the Story Barge, the girls saw Alana Yarn standing on the path. When she saw them, she gave a mysterious smile.

"This morning's activity is in a very special place," she said. "Go to the playground by the river and look for a tower. Then see if you can figure out what this morning's story is all about!"

Kirsty and Rachel exchanged excited smiles. They waved to Alana and raced off along the path to the playground.

"This is the best playground in Wetherbury," Kirsty told Rachel.

It was the biggest playground that Rachel had ever seen. There were lots of colorful swings, a mechanical merry-go-round, and seesaws, all surrounded by a bright yellow fence. There were horses on springs, jungle gyms, tunnels, and even a speaking tube. In the center of the playground was a big slide, with a tall winding ladder that led to a tower at the top.

"Do you think that's the tower Alana was talking about?" asked Kirsty.

"It must be," Rachel replied. "Come on, let's climb up and see what's at the top!"

They ran over to the ladder and climbed up. It was the tallest slide that they had ever climbed to the top of! When they reached the top, they found a small, round tower room with a small

window. Through the window they could see across the park and down the river to where the Story Barge was moored. Some other children were already inside the tower, sitting cross-legged on the floor. Each of them was busy with a sticker-activity book.

"Look, there's a pile of the activity books in the corner," said Rachel.

The girls chose one of the books and sat down to look through it together. On the cover was a picture of a tall tower with long blue hair coiling out of the high tower window.

It was so long that it reached all the way to the ground, but the person who the hair belonged to was hidden inside the tower.

"It must be Rapunzel," said Kirsty, with a little shiver of excitement. "She's one of my favorite storybook characters."

"Mine, too," said Rachel. "It's funny, though—I didn't think that she had blue hair."

She opened the book and gasped at the picture on the first page. Someone was gazing out of the tower window, but it wasn't Rapunzel. It was someone with a spiky beard, a pointy nose, and long blue hair. Rachel nudged Kirsty and showed her the page.

"Oh my goodness!" Kirsty exclaimed. "It's Jack Frost!"

Storybook Magic

Quickly, the girls flipped through the rest of the activity book.

"Every page shows a different picture of Jack Frost," Rachel said with a groan. "Where are all the pictures of Rapunzel that should be here?"

Kirsty checked the stickers in the book and looked up at Rachel with a worried expression.

"Even the stickers are pictures of Jack Frost," she said. "Look."

She held out the sticker page, where Jack Frost appeared in pose after pose, showing off his long blue hair.

"Why does no one else seem surprised by this?" Rachel wondered, looking around at the other children. "They're all just playing with the stickers."

"Let's ask them," said Kirsty, shuffling closer to a curly-haired little girl. "Excuse me, what do you think about all that blue hair?"

"Oh, it's beautiful, isn't it?" said the girl with a smile. "I wish I had long hair like that!"

"It's an amazing color," added the boy next to her. "I might ask my mom if I can dye my hair to match it."

"They haven't even noticed that it's not Rapunzel," Rachel whispered.

She and Kirsty felt worried and upset.

Jack Frost had ruined the Rapunzel story! The Storybook Fairies had explained that their magical objects gave the holder control of the stories. The fairies, of course, used their objects to make sure the stories went how they were supposed to, and ended well. But after stealing the objects, Jack Frost and his pesky goblins had actually gone *into* the stories and changed them. They wanted the stories to be all about them!

The other children were gazing down at their books again, but the girls didn't feel like looking at any more pictures of Jack Frost. Kirsty stood up and went over to the little window. She peered down at the Story Barge, wishing that she knew how to return the activity books to normal. Then, out of the corner of her eye, she saw something moving. Rosalie the Rapunzel Fairy was fluttering outside the tower, waving to her!

Kirsty turned and beckoned to Rachel, then put her finger to her lips. The other children could not be allowed to spot the little fairy. Rachel came over and smiled when she saw Rosalie.

"Hello!" she whispered. "It's great to see you again!"

Rosalie waved to them and gave a gentle smile.

Her flowing purple
gown, sparkling
with teardrop-
shaped diamonds,
swirled around her
as she fluttered
outside the
tower. Her
long blond
hair was
braided with
wildflowers,
and diamond
earrings dangled from her ears.

"Something terrible has happened," she
said. "Jack Frost has replaced Rapunzel
in her tower!"

"We know," said Kirsty, glancing back
at the activity books. "But no one other

than us seems to have noticed."

"That's because Jack Frost has my magical hairbrush," said Rosalie. "He can make as many changes as he likes, and nobody will notice."

"But *we* noticed," said Rachel.

"That's because you are such good friends to all the fairies in Fairyland," Rosalie replied. "You even carry a little magical fairy dust in your lockets. You see things that other children might not. Please, will you help me try to get my magical hairbrush back and fix the Rapunzel story? I don't think I can do it by myself."

"Of course we'll help," Kirsty responded. "But what about the other children? We can't let them see you—or your magic!"

Rosalie peeked in through the tower window.

"They are all busy looking at their activity books," she said. "Besides, the storybook world is just like Fairyland. While you are there, not a single second will pass in the human world."

With a flourish of her wand, Rosalie made a tiny purple book appear in the air above her. It floated down to rest on her outstretched hand, and the girls saw the word *Rapunzel* on the cover in golden letters.

She opened the book and a breeze ruffled the pages.

Rachel reached out to take Kirsty's hand. Even though they had already been transported into two other stories, it still felt amazing to know that they were about to travel into a book. Kirsty squeezed her hand and they shared a smile.

Rosalie tapped the tip of her wand on the open book, and some purple fairy dust sprinkled onto the pages.

19

Then she whispered:

"*Storybook magic, please come to our aid.*

Take us to where the stories are made.

Rapunzel needs help, so we cannot delay.

We must stop Jack Frost and his goblins today!"

She took a deep breath and blew the fairy dust toward Rachel and Kirsty.

It swirled and twirled through the tower window, sprinkling the girls in tiny sparkles. They closed their eyes, and felt themselves being lifted up and whisked into the book.

A Long Climb

"What's that awful noise?" cried Rachel, clapping her hands over her ears.

She opened her eyes and saw that Kirsty and Rosalie also had their hands over their ears. They were next to a tower made of smooth, white stones. It was so high that a wisp of cloud was caught on the tip of its roof. There was a single window near the top, and someone was standing there, brushing long blue hair.

"It's Jack Frost!" cried Kirsty, taking one hand away from her ear to point at the window. "And I think that noise is him trying to sing!"

It sounded like a hundred crows arguing with one another. Rosalie peered up at the window.

"I hope he's not using my magical hairbrush!" she said. "If it's in there with him, we will have to find a way to get it back."

Rachel walked around the tower. There was no door. All the way around, the wall was flat and solid. Trees surrounded the tower, and no one was in sight.

"There's only one way into this tower," Rachel said. "We'll have to fly up!"

"I can arrange that!" said Rosalie with a smile.

She waved her wand, and Rachel and Kirsty shrank to fairy size in a twinkling of fairy dust.

They fluttered their gauzy wings in delight, hovering alongside Rosalie. Together, they zoomed upward. The terrible singing got louder, and now they could hear the words.

"I'm a genius, tra-la-la.
Goblins are fools, rum-tum-tum!
Silly fairies, tra-la-la.
I'm so smart, rum-tum-tum!"

"His singing is really hurting my ears," said Rosalie. "We have to get him to stop!"

But when they were about halfway up the side of the tower, Jack Frost happened to lean out the window and look down. He spotted the fairies right away.

"What are you doing?" he yelled. "This is my story now! You can't just fly up here—you have to ask me to let down my hair! You're doing this all wrong! What's the matter with you?"

"We'll have to do what he wants, until we can get close enough to take back the hairbrush," said Kirsty.

She and Rachel looked at each other and nodded. They stopped flying upward and hovered in midair. Then, together, they said:

"Jack Frost! Jack Frost! Let down your hair!"

The long blue hair suddenly spilled out of the window, tumbling toward the fairies. They dodged out of the way just in time, but Jack swung the hair around like a whip.

"He's trying to knock us out of the air!" cried Rosalie.

She dived into the swinging blue hair and clung on as tightly as she could.

"Hold on to his hair!" she shouted. "It'll hide us!"

Kirsty and Rosalie dived into the
swishing hair beside her and hung
on with all their strength. After a few
moments, the hair stopped moving, and
the fairies heard Jack Frost cackle.

"Good riddance to those bad fairies,"
he muttered. "I showed them who's boss!
They don't dare come
near me, now that I
control the stories!
Ha, ha, ha!"

Rachel, Kirsty,
and Rosalie
exchanged grins.
Then they started
to climb the hair,
since there was no
way they could fly
among the strands of

hair. They went as slowly and quietly as they could, pulling themselves up hand over hand. It seemed to take hours, but at last they reached the windowsill. One by one, they pulled themselves up and sat on the ledge, trying to catch their breath. Then they peered into the tower room.

Jack Frost was standing with his back to the window, gazing into a mirror on the wall. His blue hair was strangely lopsided.

"Why is his hair so crooked?" Kirsty asked.

"And why is there a piece of blue elastic under his chin?" Rachel went on.

Kirsty gasped. "It's a wig!"

As they watched, Jack Frost began to brush his hair again. The brush was blue with tiny golden flowers engraved

on it. A shaft of
sunlight fell upon
it, making the
flowers gleam.

"He *is* using
my magical
hairbrush,"
said Rosalie
in a whisper.
"We have to
get it back."

"But how?" asked Rachel. "The room
is empty other than Jack Frost, and he's
holding the hairbrush. How are we going
to reach it without him seeing us?"

A Demanding Customer

Suddenly, Jack Frost whirled around and hurried over to the window.

"Come back into the room, blue hair," he said with a cackle. "You've done your work!"

There was no time for the three fairies to hide. He started to pull the hair into the room, and immediately spotted them sitting on the windowsill.

"What are you doing in here?" he screeched. "Spies! Sneaky little fairies!"

"Why are you wearing a wig?" asked Rachel, unable to control her curiosity.

Jack Frost glared at her so hard that his eyes seemed ready to pop out. His cheeks turned bright red.

"N-none of your business!" he stammered, clutching the magical hairbrush tightly. "Be quiet! I'm not staying around here to be bothered by annoying little fairies! I'm going home."

There was a bolt of icy blue magic, and Jack Frost disappeared.

"Oh, no you don't!" Rosalie exclaimed.

With a wave of her wand, the three of them were whirled upward. Words whirled around them in the air as they left the storybook world and were whisked to Fairyland. Gasping from the speed of the journey, they found themselves fluttering above the Ice Castle.

"Where did he go?" asked Rosalie.

"Listen!" said Kirsty, putting her finger to her lips.

Echoing around the snowy hillside, they could hear someone singing very out of tune.

"I've got the hairbrush, tra-la-la.
The fairies are beaten, rum-tum-tum!
They can't stop me, tra-la-la.
I am amazing, rum-tum-tum!"

"This way!" Rachel whispered.

She followed the sound of the singing toward an open window in one of the towers. Fluttering beside the window, they peeked inside. Rachel and Kirsty had seen Jack Frost's tower rooms before, and they were usually cold, gray, and drab. But this one was gleaming inside. It looked like a hair salon, with glossy surfaces, polished mirrors, and rows of curlers, combs, and brushes. Bottles of hairspray and gel lined the shelves. Through an archway, the fairies could see a supply room packed with shampoo bottles, hair combs, and lots of clips and pins.

Three goblins were working in the salon, each one dressed in a bright green uniform. While one of them was sweeping the floor, the other two were standing behind Jack Frost. He was sitting in a large chair and gazing into the mirror with a sad expression. Rosalie's magical hairbrush was still in his hand.

"I want long hair like Rapunzel's," he whined.

"We gave you long hair!" exclaimed a goblin hairdresser who had a blond fauxhawk.

He pointed to the blue wig, which was sitting on a mannequin head in front of one of the mirrors. The blue hair was coiled neatly around the head.

"I want my real hair to be long, you fool!" Jack Frost shrieked, gripping the goblin by one pointy ear.

The other hairdresser, who had a large, fake mustache, sucked in air through his teeth.

"That's tricky," he said. "We can only work with what we've got, which isn't much."

"Would you like some fashionable bangs instead?" asked the goblin hairdresser who was sweeping the floor.

"Keep out of this," snapped the goblin with the mustache.

Jack Frost shooed the blond hairdresser away. "I don't want bangs. I want long, silky hair like Rapunzel's, and I want it *now*!"

Rachel had a little shiver of excitement.

"I have an idea," she said. "I think I know how to get your magical hairbrush back, Rosalie. Follow me!"

She fluttered partway around the tower to the window of the supply room and slipped inside. When all three of them were standing among the bottles and hair

accessories, Rachel turned to Rosalie.

"Can you turn us into goblin hairdressers?" she asked in a whisper.

Rosalie looked uneasy, but she waved her wand. Instantly Rachel's and Kirsty's wings disappeared, their skin turned green, and their faces grew hard and bumpy. They were wearing the same green uniforms as the goblin hairdressers. Rachel had a mop of curly pink hair, and Kirsty had a pointy orange beard.

They looked at each other and laughed.
"I hope I don't get the giggles when
we're talking to Jack Frost," said Kirsty.
"You look so funny, Rachel!"

"Please be careful," said Rosalie. "My fairy magic is not at its full power in the Ice Castle. It might wear off!"

"Then we will just have to be quick," said Rachel in a determined voice.

A Trick and a Trip

While Rosalie hid in the supply room, Rachel and Kirsty strolled through the archway into the salon.

"Stand back!" Rachel cried in a haughty voice. "Make way! The best goblin hairdressers in the world are coming through!"

"Hey, this is our salon!" the goblin with the mustache complained.

"It's smaller than what we're used to," said Kirsty, sweeping past him to stand behind Jack Frost. "We will just have to make do! Now, Your Iciness, what sort of hairdo would you like?"

"We can do anything," Rachel added, putting her hand on his shoulder. "Long! Short! Crimped! Straight! Just say what you want and we will create it."

Jack Frost's eyes lit up.

"Really?" he asked. "Can you give me long hair like Rapunzel's?"

"No one can do that," said the blond goblin. "I've tried!"

"But you are not the greatest goblin hairdressers in the world," said Kirsty, waggling a long, bony finger at him.

"We can make all your hairstyle dreams come true!" Rachel exclaimed. "But first I need to brush out the tangles in your hair, so I will need to use your hairbrush."

She held out her hand, but Jack Frost frowned.

"My hair isn't tangled," he snapped, clutching the hairbrush to his chest.

Kirsty leaned over his shoulder and tugged at the front of his hair.

"It's full of knots!" she said.

She was hoping to distract him so that she could grab the hairbrush, but Jack Frost leaped to his feet with a yell.

"You're not hairdressers," he yelled. "You're fairies!"

Rachel and Kirsty looked up at the mirror, horrified.
Their green skin was fading, and their long noses and big feet were shrinking. As they watched, their wings appeared and their own hair replaced the goblin hairstyles.

"Sneaky, tricky, interfering fairy pests!" Jack Frost hollered, running around the salon. "You'll never get the hairbrush! Never, ever, *ever!*"

"Quick, Rachel!" cried Kirsty, grabbing the blue wig.

She threw one end of it to Rachel, just as Jack Frost charged toward the door to the castle hallway. They crouched down on either side of the door, each holding one end of the wig, and Jack Frost tripped over it as he dashed through the doorway. With a yell, he belly flopped onto the floor and the hairbrush skidded away from him. Rachel sprang over him and seized the hairbrush.

"Rosalie!" she cried.

Rosalie zoomed out of her hiding place and grabbed the magical hairbrush. She beamed with happiness as she slipped it into her pocket.

"I have it back!" she cried in a delighted voice. "I can't believe it!"

The three goblin hairdressers were glaring at the fairies with their arms folded across their chests.

"I knew they weren't the best goblin hairdressers in the world," said the goblin with the mustache. "Neither of them had a mustache."

"The best goblin hairdressers have fauxhawks, not mustaches!" squawked the blond goblin.

Squabbling, they disappeared into the supply room. The three fairies looked at Jack Frost.

"It's not fair," he said with a sniff.

He was sitting up, but his head was bowed. As they watched, his bottom lip quivered. A tear dripped down his cheek and splashed onto the floor.

"I only wanted the magical hairbrush so I could have long hair like Rapunzel's," he mumbled.

He looked so unhappy that Rachel and Kirsty felt sorry for him. They kneeled beside him, took his hands, and helped him up from the floor.

"My dreams never come true," he said

in a sad voice.

"You shouldn't have taken the hairbrush," said Kirsty. "You could have just asked Rosalie to help you."

"A fairy wouldn't help me," said Jack Frost.

Kirsty and Rachel looked at Rosalie. They knew how kind the fairies were, and they felt sure that Rosalie would want to make Jack Frost feel better.

Back to the Tower

Rosalie's eyes twinkled, and she waved
her wand. The blue wig rose up from the
floor, shook itself out, and then floated
gently onto Jack Frost's head. Jack Frost
patted his head. He wiggled it. He tugged
on the hair. And then a wide smile spread
across his face.

"It's real!" he cried. "It's really, really
real!"

He ran to one
of the salon
mirrors and
posed in front
of it, practicing
flicking his
hair over his
shoulder and
twirling it up on top of his head.

"Hey, goblins, get in here!" he hollered.
"I want hairstyles! I want hair gel! I
want combs and clips and pins! I want
braids and pigtails and ponytails! Get
to work!"

All the goblin hairdressers scurried out
of the supply room, laden down with all
the things that Jack Frost had demanded.
Rachel, Kirsty, and Rosalie looked at
one another and laughed.

"Time for us to go, I think," said Rosalie, pulling out her storybook.

When the pages opened, the three fairies were whisked inside the story once more. Fairy dust sparkled around them as they arrived back  at the bottom of the tower. Rachel and Kirsty were human again.

This time, they were not alone. A dark-haired young man was standing there, gazing up at the window. He was wearing a velvet tunic with a golden belt, and a cape swirled around his shoulders.

"It's the prince," said Rosalie in a delighted voice. "I think the story is getting back to normal."

"Rapunzel!" called the prince in a loving voice. "Rapunzel! Let down your hair!"

The girls waited, holding their breath. But there was no reply. Looking worried, the prince opened his mouth to call again, and then paused.

"Listen!" Rachel whispered.

Someone was singing in the tower. The exquisite voice rang out above them, and even the birds and butterflies flew closer to the tower to listen.

"Rapunzel is back," said Rosalie in a delighted voice.

The prince was smiling now, his eyes shining with love.

"Rapunzel!" he called again. "Rapunzel! Let down your hair!"

The girls looked up, and saw a young woman leaning over the windowsill. She smiled and waved when she saw the prince. Then her long,  silky hair tumbled down from the window, and the prince began to climb up it. Rosalie turned to the girls and gave each of them a fluttery kiss.

"Thank you for helping me get my magical hairbrush back," she said. "The story is unfolding just as it should, and it's all thanks to you."

"We're just relieved that Rapunzel and her prince are back," said Kirsty. "It's been a wonderful adventure for us."

"I will never forget your bravery and kindness," said Rosalie. "Good-bye—and thank you again!"

With a flourish of her wand, the tower, trees, and beautiful singing faded away. Kirsty and Rachel were once more in the playground tower. Around them, the other children were still playing with their sticker activity books. But now there was no sign of Jack Frost and his long blue hair. Every page and every sticker showed a scene from the original story of Rapunzel. Things were back to normal.

"How is everyone doing?" Alana asked, climbing up into the tower room. "Did you all guess the story before you saw the books?"

All the children tried to answer at once, and Alana laughed. She sat down to look at the pictures they had been completing with their stickers. Rachel picked up a spare book and turned the pages until she found the picture she wanted.

"Let's color in this scene," she said.

It was a picture of the prince reaching the tower window right after he climbed up Rapunzel's hair. The girls exchanged a happy glance and started choosing stickers.

"Alana, what happens after the prince climbs into the tower?" asked a boy.

"Rapunzel and the prince go off together to live in their own royal kingdom," said Alana. "It has a very happy ending—as all fairy tales should!"

Kirsty and Rachel smiled at each other.

"I hope there's a happy ending for all the Storybook Fairies," said Kirsty. "We still have to help Ruth the Red Riding Hood Fairy get her magical object back from Jack Frost and the goblins."

"We will," said Rachel, as she colored in the prince's velvet tunic. "Like Alana said, all fairy tales have happy endings!"

Kirsty grinned. She couldn't wait to help Ruth find her magic basket.

RAINBOW magic

THE STORYBOOK FAIRIES

Rachel and Kirsty found Elle's,
Mariana's, and Rosalie's missing magic
objects. Now it's time for
them to help

Ruth
the Red Riding Hood Fairy!

Join their next adventure in
this special sneak peek …

Fairy Tale in the Firelight

"There's something so magical about a campfire," said Kirsty Tate, warming her hands as the flames flickered.

"I love staring into the flames," said her best friend, Rachel Walker. "If you look at them for long enough, you can start to see pictures in there."

The girls leaned against each other, feeling happy, sleepy, and relaxed. They had spent a wonderful weekend at the Wetherbury Storytelling Festival, but now it was Sunday evening and the fun was nearly at an end. Together with the other children from the festival, they were sitting on logs in a circle around a campfire. Alana Yarn, one of their favorite authors, had helped organize the weekend, and she was sitting on a log, too. The girls had had a wonderful time getting to know her.

"So," said Alana, looking around the circle at them all. "Have you enjoyed the Storytelling Festival? What was the best part?"

Everyone nodded and started to call out their favorite moments.

"The only bad thing about the whole weekend is that it has to end," said Rachel.

Alana smiled.

"We still have one more storytelling session before you have to go home," she said.

There was a large wicker basket in front of her, and she began to rummage through it. Rachel turned and smiled at Kirsty.

"Thank you for inviting me to stay this weekend," she said. "It was a great idea to come to the Storytelling Festival—I've had an amazing time."

"You're welcome," said Kirsty. "I'm

really glad you came. I like everything ten times more when you're here. It's been an extra-special weekend."

Rachel nodded. "Especially because we've had such a wonderful time with the Storybook Fairies," she whispered.

Rachel and Kirsty had shared lots of secret adventures with fairies, and meeting the Storybook Fairies had been enchanting. Elle the Thumbelina Fairy had whisked them away to the Fairyland Library, where they met Mariana the Goldilocks Fairy, Rosalie the Rapunzel Fairy, and Ruth the Red Riding Hood Fairy. The fairies were all very upset because Jack Frost and his goblins had stolen their magical objects, but Kirsty and Rachel had already helped get three of the objects back.

"I just hope that we can get Ruth's magical basket back soon," said Kirsty. "Until then, Jack Frost still has control of her story."

RAINBOW magic™

Which Magical Fairies Have You Met?

- ☐ The Rainbow Fairies
- ☐ The Weather Fairies
- ☐ The Jewel Fairies
- ☐ The Pet Fairies
- ☐ The Sports Fairies
- ☐ The Ocean Fairies
- ☐ The Princess Fairies
- ☐ The Superstar Fairies
- ☐ The Fashion Fairies
- ☐ The Sugar & Spice Fairies
- ☐ The Earth Fairies
- ☐ The Magical Crafts Fairies
- ☐ The Baby Animal Rescue Fairies
- ☐ The Fairy Tale Fairies
- ☐ The School Day Fairies

3190106014 4872

■SCHOLASTIC

Find all of your favorite fairy friends at
scholastic.com/rainbowmagic

RMFAIRY15